PROCUREMENT

Kathy McLelland

Edited by Gloria J. Phillips

NEW HARBOR PRESS

RAPID CITY, SD

McLelland/New Harbor Press
1601 Mt. Rushmre Rd, Ste 3288
Rapid City, SD 57701
www.NewHarborPress.com

Publisher's Note: This is a work of fiction. Names, characters,
places, and incidents are a product of the author's imagination.
Locales and public names are sometimes used for atmospheric
purposes. Any resemblance to actual people, living or dead,
or to businesses, companies, events, institutions, or locales is
completely coincidental.

Ordering Information:
Quantity sales. Special discounts are available on quantity pur-
chases by corporations, associations, and others. For details,
contact the "Special Sales Department" at the address above.

Procurement / Kathy McLelland. -- 1st ed.
Edited by Gloria J. Phillips

ISBN 978-1-63357-451-9

FOREWORD

WHILE THE CHARACTERS AND story line in this novel are purely fictional, my friend and sister in Christ, Kathy McLelland, was inspired to tell the story of the unknown and unwanted children in our society. It is hard for those of us who were reared by loving and nurturing parents, to even imagine a scenario like the one depicted here. But, in fact, there are all kinds of subcultures that are little known to the general public. And while we live in the world of "I don't want to be involved," someone has to stand up for those who cannot stand up for themselves. Thank you, Kathy, for telling their story.

David W. McNary
Pastor, Retired

CHAPTER 1

ELIZABETH CONNALLY STEPPED CARE-FULLY from the backseat of the long black vehicle and raised her eyes to view the splendorous blue sky above her. She felt the sun's intrusive August heat.

"No rain today," she muttered to herself as her driver, William Hudson handed her the walking cane upon which she was growing more and more dependent. "Thank you, William," she said as he lent her the support of his arm.

"Please wait here" she said, bringing her gaze directly in line with his.

"But madam…" he began.

She quickly cut him off and turned toward the gate. "No need, no need," she repeated as she stepped upon the familiar winding pavement that would eventually take her to where she wanted to be on this hot August day.

As she neared her destination, she noticed that a small stuffed brown bear which had been badly weathered by the elements had fallen over at the base of a headstone. Leaning upon her cane, she stooped to place the little stuffed toy back in its original position before walking on.

She soon reached the sprawling live oak tree which over the years had become a comforting friend to her, lending its branches to shade her from the sun and be a partner in her grief. An iron bench that had been placed beneath the tree many years before caught her weight as she sat down. She looked across the grave and the now yellowed pink roses in the ornate iron vase. Above it was the familiar statue of a child, a smiling little girl holding a bird in her hands. Tears began to sting her eyes and then streamed freely down her cheeks. She removed her sunglasses revealing ice blue eyes to the sunlight and wiped her tears, but to no avail as the tears continued. The heat of the summer morning was too much for her and her stomach began to heave. She arose and as she did so, the nausea overcame her and leaning upon her cane, she vomited. Her knees buckled and she would have fallen had Hudson's strong arm not caught her.

Let's go home, Madam," he said as he guided her to the paved path which led back to the car.

"But the roses," she whimpered, gesturing to the new pink roses on the bench.

"I will return and all will be done as you wish," he said.

"If only it could have been as I had wished. God forgive me. God forgive us all. She would have been twenty-one years old today" she whispered.

Yes, ma'am," he replied.

CHAPTER TWO

ELENA GARRETT TURNED OFF the screaming alarm at 5 a.m., knocking her phone to the floor, she quietly got out of her bed and reached for her robe. She tiptoed toward the kitchen as she lit a cigarette. She put on the coffee pot and looked in the refrigerator for anything edible. Finding nothing but a carton of old Chinese takeout and something that might have once been a piece of fruit, she slammed the refrigerator door. Turning, she walked down the short hall to her daughter's bedroom.

"Time to get up, Sweetie," she said gently to the sleeping child, who arose rubbing her eyes.

Celena stumbled back into the bedroom and dressed for the workday. Blue jeans and a tee shirt were all that was required at the small store where she worked standing at a check out center making change for people purchasing cigarettes and lottery tickets. Thousands of dollars passed through her hands each day, but none of it was hers. She barely made enough money to pay her rent and buy food for the two of them to eat. Some nights their supper was a bag of chips and a bottle of milk which they shared.

It had not always been such a sparse diet for them. Celena's husband and Gracie's father had changed so much under the pressure of the last three years. One night, he went out with friends and simply had never returned. He called two days later and said that he would not be back, and that she could do whatever she wanted about belongings, their marriage and even Gracie. Celena knew that Gracie's birth had been too much responsibility for Jack, who was only twenty years old when they married. Gracie came along a year after their marriage despite using birth control and Jack never fully accepted the "burden" of fatherhood. Soon after Gracie's birth, being a husband didn't seem to appeal too much to him either. He would go out by himself at night leaving Celena to care for the new baby who like all normal infants, cried at night. Sometimes he would be gone for days. So, Celena was not surprised by the coldness in his voice when he told her that he would not be coming back.

"Good riddance," she said to herself, one less mouth to feed." Celena had enough to deal with raising one child.

Gracie had issues with colic. Sometimes she would cry even after Celena had given her the medicine that would eventually ease her pain. After giving the baby her medicine, Celena would hold Gracie tightly to her. Some nights she would sing and even pray when the baby's pain seemed worse than usual. Those were hard nights for both mother and child, but they also were the times that bonded Gracie and Celena more than Celena could understand. Sometimes, she cried when she looked down at the sleeping baby in her arms, wondering at Gracie's peaceful beauty and listening to her steady even breathing after the colic had eased and the crying ceased. Even though Celena was exhausted and would get little or no sleep that night, somehow her strength multiplied deep within her bones, and she was able to finish the coming workday.

Celena did not understand the depth of her bond to Gracie. She thought that she had forgotten how to sing hymns and pray as she did with Gracie in her arms on hard nights. Yet, when she needed her faith, somehow it welled up from deep within her along with a mother's love which sometimes overwhelmed her heart. The faith that she had as a child was still there within her soul, buried deeply, but still there. That was so long ago, she thought.

Just then Gracie came toddling down the hallway jarring Celena away from her thoughts.

"Mommie," she said, rubbing her eyes.

Celena picked her up for a quick morning cuddle before the long day began. Gracie's size threes were getting noticeably tight as Celena quickly dressed her and readied her for the day at Mrs. Reiner's across the hall. Gracie was almost four years old. She could go to daycare, but Celena avoided the state-run day cares which really were not as inexpensive as they professed to be... not by the time you paid for lunch and a midday snack. Mrs. Reiner charged Celena only five dollars per day and said it was easier to cook for two than one anyway, so lunch and cookies were included in the five-dollar charge. Mrs. Reiner had been a teacher before she had retired, and Celena suspected that she really enjoyed having Gracie around.

Celena thought Mrs. Reiner probably would have kept Gracie for nothing had she not insisted on paying something to keep her five and sometimes six days each week if she could get some overtime hours.

Winter was coming and heat must be paid for so Gracie would not get sick. Celena always hated taking Gracie into the Health Clinic in her neighborhood. The nurse always asked her because of her low-income status if she wished to procure a "release" for Gracie, assuming that Celena would have a better life for herself without having to be saddled with a sickly little daughter. Just the mention of it always made Celena's blood run cold. Giving up her daughter would be like turning out the last light in her life. There would be only darkness.

Celena gently rushed Gracie down the hall as though she was a mother hen shooing her chick. Just as she was about to knock on Mrs. Reiner's door, the sweet older lady opened it and greeted them both with her usual warm smile. She handed Celena a cup of coffee and then took Gracie by the hand.

"Go and eat your breakfast, Darling. It's on the table."

"See you, Mommie," said Gracie as she kissed Celena and did as Mrs. Reiner instructed.

"See you, Baby," returned Celena.

 Would you mind if I took Gracie to a meeting at my church this afternoon? We are planning a special program for the service next week. I'm sure there will be other children there so Gracie might even make a new friend. We will be back before you get off work."

"No problem," answered Celena, glancing at her watch, "see you tonight."

CHAPTER THREE

CELENA ENTERED THE SMALL cottage on the park green with only two minutes to spare before she would be docked a quarter hour on the timeclock. She quickly retrieved her timecard and punched it before putting down her purse.

"I thought you weren't gonna make it, Sweet Cheeks," muttered the old lady known to Celena and the other young girls in the small shop as "Old Rose."

Old Rose worked the graveyard shift from six p.m. until six in the morning. It always amazed Celena how many people actually bought coffee, magazines and lottery tickets in the middle of the night. Some gambled on the machines in the store, too. It seemed like there was never a peaceful or quiet time in the part of the city in which Celena and Gracie lived. Celena longed for the day that she could move away from the urban rush and constant movement of the city life.

Suddenly, the front door burst open and the other girl who worked in the shop hurried to the time clock and with a quick motion, retrieved and punched her timecard.

"Made it," she said.

"Just barely," grumbled Old Rose as she brushed by Merilee, and left for the day.

"Old witch," said Merilee with her usual flippant brand of malice. She winked at Celena as she said it as though it made it a little less hateful, but Celena was already reading the day's headline in the one morning paper that the shop now carried. Almost everything had gone cyber and all papers were gone now except for the one that she was reading. Celena could not afford the price of internet or computers, so this was her connection to the world around her. It irritated Merrilee that Celena had missed the whole interaction between Rose and herself.

Celena was too busy looking for a better job in the classified advertisements for employment within the newspaper, something she did every morning. She so desperately needed to improve her financial situation. Their apartment was small, but quite nice and Celena did not know how much longer she could manage to pay the rent and utilities and buy enough food for herself and Gracie. Food and electricity was costing a little more each month. She had already received a letter from the investment group that owned her building that informed her that rent would be going up in January of the next year. It was late summer now, but soon the season would give way to fall and in no time the oncoming need for more expensive heat in their apartment would require more money from her pocket.

Celena's mother, who called frequently to check on her, had told her just yesterday that she was amazed at how strong Celena had become since Jack had left. Her parents were strong Christians and encouraged her to wait before seeking a divorce from Jack. They would like to see Celena's family remain intact. Her mom talked a lot about forgiveness for Jack. Celena was so angry at him in the beginning because she felt betrayed and deserted. However, instead of her heart growing hard and cold after the anger subsided, she still longed for Jack. She so desperately needed him, needed his support for the family and especially his love that seemed so wonderful at first...

"What in the world are you thinking?" interrupted Merilee into Celena's thoughts.

"Thinking about Jack," she returned before actually considering who she was talking to.

"For Pete's sake, Celena" The jerk is gone. Move on."

It was Merilee's philosophy that Celena complicated her life by loving everybody too much. Everyone meant Jack, her parents and sometimes Celena thought, even Gracie. This was hard to understand as Merilee was a mother herself. Her little boy, Dawson, was about Gracie's age. Merilee had told Celena early on in their friendship that she did not know who Dawson's father was. She said it could be one of three men and if she ever needed to know she would use her parent's money to find out which one it was.

Dawson was an amazingly sweet child despite the lack of motherly affection he received from his mother. Merilee moved from man to man with no concern for the effect it had on Dawson.

Celena listened to Merilee's stories about her nightlife and her newest male partner and sometimes worried for Dawson. She knew that he spent a lot of time with Merilee's parents, sometimes for several nights in a row. However, she did know that they loved their grandson and were glad for the time with him. Merilee also realized that her parents adored the boy and instead of that love warming her heart, somehow it seemed to make her have a kind of seething jealousy, just below a superficial layer of denial.

Merilee once told Celena that the only reason that she held down a job was that her father insisted that she contribute something to provide for little Dawson. Celena had met Merilee's parents and wondered how two such nice people raised a daughter who did not seem too interested in being a parent herself.

Celena's thoughts snapped back to what Merilee had said and responded to Merilee by telling her that she was moving on from Jack, just not at the speed of light.

"Well, you ought to think about moving a little faster sister, said Merilee. I saw Jack at Reno's last night, and he made it plain to see that he has moved on."

Celena swiveled her chair toward Merilee so quickly that she knocked her coffee cup over, spilling coffee all over the counter and the newspaper that she was attempting to read. She felt as though her heart had turned over as well but managed to ask calmly how Jack appeared.

Merilee reported that he appeared to be reeling drunk or high and that he seemed to be there with some woman with long red hair. Celena figured that this was Karen Fuller, a former neighbor in their apartment building. Karen seemed to gravitate toward Jack at parties and even when they ran into each other in the hall or elevator. Celena and Karen had always been cordial to one another, but Celena thought Karen might have more than a feeling of neighborly cordiality toward Jack.

"Did you hear what I said, Celena?" demanded Merilee wishing she could shake Celena and wake her up to the reality of Jack's unfaithfulness. But deep in her soul, Merilee also wished that she could have the same kind of loving spirit, patient and full of compassion that Celena had even when she had been so hurt.

"I heard you," replied Celena as she looked up to see her first customer of the morning. He ordered coffee, a newspaper, and bought two lottery tickets. Thankfully, the morning became quite busy with customers and there was no more time to talk to Merilee or to think about Jack.

CHAPTER FOUR

JACK GARRETT AWOKE THE next morning on the floor of the bathroom in the house that he and Karen Fuller had been sharing since he had left Celena and Gracie six months ago. He was lying in a pool of his own vomit and urine. The vestiges of a night spent drinking and shooting up. He got up and his head began to reel. This was not the first time Jack felt the nausea and dizziness. He knew what to do. He got to his knees over the toilet and put his fingers down his throat. The vomit came and the cramping in his stomach ceased. He hung there on the toilet until the dizziness subsided and tried, this time successfully to stand up. Stripping the nasty clothing from his body, he stepped into the shower and turned on the water. It came blasting toward his chest ice cold. Cursing, he tried the hot water again. Nobody paid the gas bill, he surmised. Not the first time. It wasn't as though there was not enough money. Karen was a very successful self-taught street chemist/pusher who brewed the best "ink" in the city. She had so many customers that she could not keep them supplied. She produced the colored concoction on the east side of the city in a warehouse rented specifically for the purpose. Ink had not been deemed illegal yet and might never become so given the relaxation of all the "Freedom to Ingest" laws that had been passed by the government when Jack was only a child. The problem was that she had become a user of late and couldn't remember to pay her household bills. Jack wondered if she had remembered her way home from Reno's last night. She had been "writing" a lot of Ink the previous evening as well as doing business in the club. Jack knew that sometimes she would go to the warehouse to close pending deals before coming home.

His question was answered as soon as he opened the bedroom door. Karen lay sprawled across the bed, still in the clothes she wore to Reno's the night before. Jack pushed her over on her side of the bed and climbed in beside her. He noticed her bare arm that had fallen across the pillow above her head. She had been writing with the Ink which was what some users did. Ink was injected just under the skin which was just what many people wanted to do. The time after injecting the Ink until its first effects were felt was about an hour. That gave users a chance to get where they were going clear-headed before the hit of the ink was felt. That was one reason for its popularity. The other is that Karen, unlike other street pushers topped-off the injectables with different colors of ink used in tattooing. It was the trend of her fashionable users to make a design over time with the small dots of ink left after the effects of the drug had worn off. This was what Karen called "writing." He had noticed that Karen had begun writing something on her own forearm. Probably a dollar sign, he thought, and then sleep overtook him.

CHAPTER 5

AFTER LUNCH, MRS. REINER and Gracie took a short bus ride to Parkview Church where Mrs. Reiner had attended since she was a young bride. Mrs. Reiner and her husband had enjoyed many years of learning of God's grace and mercy toward them and enjoyed the close fellowship with other believers like themselves. Now that her husband had passed on, her church was even more comforting to Nola, as she was known to her friends.

Nola pushed open the heavy door leading to the basement meeting area and Gracie walked through carrying a bag of dolls and a coloring book. Nola ushered Gracie into a small room adjoining the area where the meeting was about to begin. Two other girls and a little boy were already playing, and Gracie sat down on the floor and joined them. When Nola walked into the meeting room an older gentleman at the table gave her his seat and went to get another chair for himself. When he was seated the tall young blond woman at the head of the table began the meeting. She was wearing nurse scrubs and appeared tired from a long workday.

"And what about Lizzie?" she began. "Will she be here today?"

One of the other ladies at the table reminded Nurse Linda Norris that this was the twentieth anniversary of Beth's procurement and it had been especially hard on Lizzie this year.

"I called yesterday," said Mrs. Reiner, "just to remind her about today's committee meeting." She went on to say that she had spoken with Hudson, Mrs. Connally's personal assistant, and he had said that since her visit to the cemetery in late August, she had not spoken much. She stayed to herself, accompanied only by her dog either within her home or in her private garden located on the back of her property. He said that she was currently not accepting any visitors.

"I know that she has not been at church in quite a while. It sounds as if a visit is exactly what she needs, whether she wants one or not. Who will volunteer to go?" asked Linda.

Mrs. Reiner said that she and maybe even Gracie would pay her a visit within the next few days. Maybe seeing Gracie would give Lizzie a small glimmer of sunshine. Maybe Gracie could charm Hudson into letting them through the front door to visit with Lizzie.

Nola Reiner also said that it grew harder and harder not to tell Lizzie that Beth had been rescued from procurement and in just a few months, the sanction of safety would be over. Beth would have the chance to contact someone from her past if she so wished.

"I think it would help Lizzie just to know that Beth is not dead, even if she never got to see her face to face or hold her in her arms," remarked Mrs. Reiner. I just hope she lives long enough to see the day..." she whispered under her breath.

The meeting began and Linda reported to the committee that no new procurements had been requested during the last month.

"Praise God," said Nola and the others echoed her words.

Linda interrupted to say that there had been three new receptors enrolled in two different regions in the participating churches. Becoming a receptor was a delicate process requiring much time to complete. Three receptors at once were an unheard of blessing.

The group prayed together praising God that there had been no new procurements in their community and for the enrollment of the receptor families. After discussing the plans for the next church social gathering, the meeting was adjourned.

The group spent the rest of the afternoon visiting and enjoying the laughter of the children who were playing together. Rose had managed to make a cake that morning even though she probably gave up her sleep to do so. Nola made coffee and they shared the cake. Mr. Johnson, the only gentleman at the gathering that day, took strawberry ice cream from the freezer in the kitchen and served the children far too large portions. After he had served the children, he sat down beside Nola and quietly asked her why Elizabeth Connally had been kept in the dark about her granddaughter. Nola explained to him that Mrs. Connally, or Lizzie as she was known to her friends, had only recently joined the group. Mr. Johnson was also a newer member of the group.

Nola told him that it had not been an easy decision, but the sanction of safety could not be breached for any child, not even for Lizzie Connally's granddaughter. It would be dangerous for the group if word ever got out and it might make it impossible to place children saved from a procurement procedure. Children who grew up with receptor families must remain anonymous until they became legal adults. It was up to receptor parents to tell their children the truth or not. Some children who were close to five years of age when they endured the Procurement process might have some lingering memories of their birth parents. Some might want to find a biological relative. Some might not ever want to see them again.

"I understand," replied Bill. "But it still seems heartless to let Lizzie suffer when the child is alive".

Rose, who had been silent up to now, stood up and said, "Bill, we hope and pray that Beth is alive. But the truth is we don't know if she is or isn't. She could have died in an accident or from an illness."

"You don't know whether she is dead or alive!" He exclaimed.

Silence gripped the room. No one said anything. Then Nola rose slowly and said simply, "There is no trail left for the government or birth families to trace between us and the receptors." We have faith that a life that was supposed to have suffered an early and merciless end was rescued from such a fate. It is enough. It must be enough. The more anonymity and distance, the more safety there is for everyone involved. We have been placing children for twenty-three years and we do not contact receptors, nor do they contact us after placement. We have never met or have knowledge of any of the children that have been rescued. We don't have to. We trust God. We have faith that He blesses our efforts and the children.

"We'll just save all the joyous reunions for heaven," said Rose as she put on her coat to leave.

"Let's go home, Gracie," said Nola Reiner.

Linda cleaned the kitchen and then as the day was turning into early evening, she donned her jacket against the increasing coolness of the October wind and left.

There would be another meeting of the "Parkview Church Social Planning Committee" in thirty days.

CHAPTER 6

MERILEE COOPER ARRIVED HOME after her twelve-hour shift to find her mother holding her four-year-old son, Dawson. Dawson had a fever and had been crying, saying that his ear hurt all afternoon. Mrs. Cooper had finally decided that she should take Dawson to the Madison St. Clinic where he could receive treatment. Merilee saw by her mother's face and the clinic's statement on the table that her mother knew what Merilee had done concerning Dawson.

Merilee knew her mother would be furious with her, so she feigned an excuse of leaving her purse in the car and tried to go back out of the front door. Mrs. Cooper laid the now relieved and sleeping child down on the sofa and turned toward her daughter.

"What have you done, Merilee? The nurse said there were procurement papers in the process of government approval for Dawson. She assumed I knew about this because I was on his privacy agreement, which evidently, you have forgotten," she said in a frantic voice.

"Have you lost your mind? I had to pay three times the normal cost for Dawson's treatment. I probably couldn't have gotten treatment at all had Dawson not been screaming the whole time and it became clear to them that I could pay and was not leaving until something was done for him. All they would offer us at first was a drug to make him sleep. They put a high price on antibiotic, but I paid it, Merilee. I paid it and now he can get well. I swear to you, Merilee, you better not procure this child or..."

"Or what? You'll cut me out of your will? I thought that was already done. Anyway, he's my kid and it's my choice, she said. Like it or not."

"I won't let you kill this child," said Mrs. Cooper. I'm taking him with me tonight. You've lost your mind, and I won't let you do this."

"And I'll have you arrested in an hour. For once in my life, the choices are mine. Get out!" Merilee screamed.

"I won't let it be, Merilee" returned her mother in a low voice.

"Don't you threaten me, Mother". You're no better. Remember, I'm your second daughter. You killed your first one. What was her name? Or did they even bother to give aborted babies a name in those days?"

Joanna Cooper felt the tears sting her cheeks. Her hands began to tremble, and she felt a rush of nausea. Somehow this young woman who was her daughter and whom she had loved and worried about for twenty-six years stood now before her as her judge, jury and worst of all, her accuser.

"How...?" Joanna began.

"How did I find out?" asked Merilee.

"Records, Mother. They keep good ones, she said as she reached into her pocket, retrieved a cigarette and lit it. It was on the family history sheet that came with the procurement packet," said Merilee coldly.

Joanna reached for her coat. She knelt over her grandson and a choking sob escaped her throat.

"Oh, Dawson, I'm so sorry...I'm so sorry", she repeated over and over.

"Don't make me sick!" said Merilee. You have no right to judge me. You aren't a fit grandmother. You aren't even a fit mother. Now get out!"

Joanna kissed her sleeping grandson and walked past Merilee saying nothing. She paused at the door as though she would speak, but changing her mind, she walked through the doorway and closed the door softly, gently, behind her, walking out into the darkness that waited to receive her grief, sorrow and guilt.

CHAPTER 7

CELENA KNOCKED ON MRS. Reiner's door at six-thirty in the evening, her usual time. Mrs. Reiner opened the door and invited Celena in for supper, which was a great relief as she recalled the sad contents of her refrigerator earlier that morning. The aroma of cooking food coming from the kitchen made her remember that she was ravenous. She gladly accepted the invitation and joined Gracie in the living room.

"I'd love to help you," called out Celena to Nola who busied herself in the kitchen.

"Nonsense, you just rest and love your baby. I am sure that you have been on your feet all day," replied Nola.

Gracie was already climbing up into her mommy's lap for a hug. Celena wrapped her tired arms around Gracie and told her that she would not have to go to work tomorrow and that they would get to spend the whole day together. Gracie squeezed Celena tightly around the neck and laid her head on Celena's shoulder.

"I missed you, Mommy," she said softly.

"I know, Baby. I missed you too. But tomorrow we will sleep late and go out for donuts for breakfast and go to the park if it isn't raining and ..."

"Supper's ready!" called Nola.

The three of them enjoyed the meal and Celena and Gracie returned home for an early bedtime. Celena had no idea as she went to bed that night that tomorrow would bring the beginning of changes to her life. Without dreaming, she slept softly, peacefully.

CHAPTER 8

CELENA WAS IN THE kitchen the next morning, pouring a cup of coffee for herself, when she heard a soft knock at the door. Thinking it was Mrs. Reiner, she walked to the door in her pajamas, barefoot, expecting to see Nola's smiling face when she opened it.

She almost dropped the cup of hot coffee in her hand when she opened the door. A strong hand reached in to keep it from spilling all over her and dropping to the floor.

"Jack!" She choked. "What are you doing here? I never..."

I know, you didn't expect to see me today or maybe, ever. Celena, if you could just let me see Gracie's face... hear her voice. I think I could be okay. Please, even if she doesn't see me. Just for a second" he begged.

Before Celena could even respond, Gracie came from the hallway and ran toward Jack, jumping into his arms. Tears streamed down his face as she said "Daddy, my Daddy"!

Celena caught enough breath to bid Jack to come in and she shut the door behind him. She sat down on the sofa and let Gracie have this moment as she tried to figure out what her own feelings were. She considered screaming but did not feel that she needed to be rescued. She inhaled as if to speak but no words would come. All at once, all of her energy drained from her, and she sat limply on the sofa as father and daughter talked. Thoughts came racing back from the night he left... the desperation she felt and then, the anger. But saying nothing, she could only listen as Jack and Gracie spoke quietly to one another. It reminded her of other times when she had seen them together, loving each other, laughing, enjoying being together. But then the anger interrupted. How could he think that all he had to do was knock on the door, walk back in and just take up where he left off. She and Gracie had grown so close since he had been gone, almost a year now. She resented his holding her daughter. She was about to tell him to go when Gracie turned her glowing face toward her and asked if Jack could go to the park and eat breakfast with them. Before Celena could think of a response, Jack, reading Celena's face, said that he could not. He said that he had to go to work at his new job and would go next time. Gracie, disappointed, climbed down from Jack's lap and went to Celena. "Go, get dressed so we can leave, Love. Tell Daddy you will see him next time."

Gracie hugged Jack and went back to her room to get dressed in the clothes Celena had laid out for her. Jack got up and headed for the door. Before he left, he turned to Celena, and said simply, "Thank you," closing the door behind himself.

Celena realized that she was still holding the cup of coffee in her hand, which was now shaking.

How, she thought, could I stand there and not say anything? I have thought about this time when I would get to have my say, finally...finally, get to tell him what a sorry excuse for a husband and father he has been to me and especially to Gracie. Instead, I said nothing. Tears came. Her anger subsided and before she could explore it further, she heard Gracie say, Mommy, I'm ready. Where's Daddy? I brought him Mr.

Scruggles to take back with him. He can hold him for a while.

Mr. Scruggles was a well-worn bear that Jack had brought home to Gracie when she was barely three years old.

Clearly, Gracie held no malice in her sweet child's heart for her father. Celena, however, was having none of Jack's lies. She had enough before he left. She remembered Jack leaning over Karen, laughing, his arm around her, no remorse, no thoughts of Gracie, then... the tears dried up and the anger returned that she now knew was just below the surface. She had thought it was buried.

"I'll have to get a bigger shovel," she muttered to herself.

She and Gracie sat in the park and ate donuts. While watching Gracie run and play on the merry-go-round with two other children, Celena regained her thoughts.

Along with her thoughts, came questions about her reaction to Jack. She figured that she would feel only anger...but there was something else. Maybe a little mercy? Things were hard for them after Gracie's birth. But she toughed it out. Why couldn't he? He left them. Case closed. He left them. But then, Gracie's face and her joy at seeing Jack again. What right had she to stand in the way of Gracie having her dad, even if it were just for a short visit. Somehow, seeing Jack made Gracie's day full of joy and hope. It left Celena worn out and questioning her own will for the two of them to make it without him.

Later, that evening as she was turning out her light to go to sleep, all the anger tucked neatly back into its place, she wondered if perhaps someone else's will might be bringing Jack back and softening Celena's heart. Someone's will that was working through a little girl's love to restore their family.

She asked God for blessings over Gracie and expressed gratefulness for Mrs. Reiner and her job but stayed away from talking to God about her heart. She wasn't ready for that yet.

CHAPTER NINE

THE MID-NOVEMBER WIND WHIPPED round about them as Nola and Gracie got off the bus a few blocks from Elizabeth Connally's home. Nola took Gracie's earmuffs from her bag and put them over Gracie's thermal cap to give her extra protection from the wind. She wrapped her own muffler tightly around her neck and began the short walk to Lizzie's house. She had not forgotten that she was elected to pay Lizzie a visit and inquire about Lizzie's absence from church and "club" meetings.

Gracie tried hard to match Nola step for step as they ascended the steps to the Connally mansion. She asked if she could ring the doorbell and Nola nodded.

Surprisingly, it was not Hudson who answered the door, but Lizzie herself along with her pet Great Dane. Gracie was very impressed by the huge dog, and this seemed to touch Lizzie. She invited them into the entryway. Through the cracked door on the sitting room, they heard Hudson talking on the phone.

The dog made a successful run from the foyer to the library with Gracie on his heels.

"What's his name?" asked Gracie giggling and petting the dog at the same time.

Clearly, Lizzie was charmed by Gracie's fascination with her beloved dog.

"Sir Percival is his name, but we just call him Percy," she called out with a laugh.

Hudson seemed startled and ended his phone conversation abruptly by saying he would call again.

Gracie patted Percy, motioning with her other hand and calling, "Come on puppy." They walked victoriously from the room to rejoin Lizzie and Nola in the foyer.

Lizzie led the group into the library and asked Hudson to bring refreshments. Gracie sat on the floor with Percy's giant head in her small lap. The huge canine was basking in all the attention, leaving Nola and Lizzie to talk.

Pleasantries were exchanged, but Nola knew that she was on a mission to see how Lizzie really was doing. She was caring, but direct and asked why Lizzie was absent from church and club meetings. Lizzie explained what Nola already knew about Beth and her friend's grief over her loss, still present after twenty years. Nola listened compassionately to her friend as she explained the guilt that she felt for not trying to intervene in her own daughter's procurement request for Beth. She confessed that she never thought her daughter Kim would really go through with it. It was unthinkable. However, Lizzie was unaware of the depth of drug addiction her daughter had succumbed to. She said that her daughter proceeded quickly with the procurement process, and it was over before Lizzie knew it had taken place. She was very angry with Kim for many months but eventually, made peace with her daughter, only to have Kim perish from a drug overdose a year later.

Nola's heart broke for Lizzie, and she wanted so badly to give her news about Beth. But she remembered what Rose had said at the meeting. There was no way to contact Beth. It had been so many years since she had been rescued that anything could have happened. Beth could be alive or dead. If she was still alive and was made aware of her past next year on her twenty-first birthday, it would be her choice to walk back to her family, a family she might view as deserting her and buying her death.

Nola was right. Lizzie might have to wait until Heaven for a joyful reunion with Beth.

Nola hugged her friend and offered condolences but reminded Lizzie that she was now part of the effort to save innocent lives that were being procured by selfishness and cruelty. She was needed back at the forefront of the battle. Her presence was missed. Her perspective and help gave others in the group courage and a will to continue in what could be considered interfering with government and the law. How saving life could be a crime was unimaginable, but sadly, a fact in this day and time.

Gracie interrupted politely that Percy needed some milk as she and the ladies drank tea. Lizzie smiled and summoned Hudson who brought a dog treat the size of Gracie's shoe to the dog. Gracie was thrilled to please her new friend. Lizzie was comforted by Gracie's presence. All and all, the day was good.

Curiously, Hudson was on the phone again as the ladies exited the foyer. Nola noticed that he seemed nervous but made no more of it. She heard only a few words, and they made her wonder if Elizabeth Connally had been honest with her...medical transport will be necessary, yes, I understand. Was Lizzie sick? Seriously ill? As she was about to turn around and ask Lizzie, the door closed softly.

"Next time," she whispered under her breath and prayed a simple prayer for her friend.

Mercifully, they only had to wait at the bus stop for a couple of minutes. The temperature was dropping. The snow was beginning to fall. Winter was coming.

CHAPTER TEN

LINDA NORRIS WOKE UP on a cold December morning and made coffee. She took her Bible and sat down at her kitchen table. The marker for her daily reading was still in place from yesterday. She turned the page to Psalms 36, but paused before she began to read, events of the day intruding on her thoughts. There was to be a Procurement carried out this day on a little girl who was only twenty-two months old. The little girl suffered with Cystic Fibrosis. The case folder lay on the table next to her Bible. Inside, was a description of the child.

Name: Victoria G.

Age: 22 months and 3 days at date of Procurement Procedure

Physical Description: Weight: 19 lbs. 8 oz. Height: 30 in

Hair: Brown

Eyes: Blue

Procurement Procedure Date: December 1....

Today, thought Linda. The first day of the month of Christmas.

"Well, it won't be the last day of this sweet one's life," she determined. There had been special plans made for this little angel and she was about to go on a long journey towards care and medication and hopefully more years of a better life.

She thought that her Bible reading was perfect for this day not just for herself, but Victoria, too.

Sing unto the Lord a new song.

Sing unto the Lord, all the earth,

Sing unto the Lord, bless his name.

Shew forth his salvation from day to day.

Declare his glory among the heathen,

His wonders among all the people.

For the Lord is great, and greatly to be praised:

He is to be feared above all gods.

For all the gods of the nations are idols:

But the Lord made the heavens.

Linda prayed and thanked God for His great mercy and loving care. She asked for strength and God's hand to guide hers as she played her part in the plan to help Victoria begin a new life today.

She dressed quickly, donning her scrubs and shoes. She always left early on the day of any procurement procedure just to make sure that she was prepared. Often, the doctor signed off on the procedure, inspected medications and then left the rest of the "work" to the nurse in charge. Today, she was the one in charge. She had already calculated with care the exact dosage needed to produce sleep very close to death, but not entirely. Usually, the doctor did not check for final vitals. The nurse did this and then reported to the doctor with death certificate in hand for him to finish. She was ready. Nothing was written down. Dosage was only in her mind. Nothing on paper. Not even a note on the inside of her hand. No paper trail was the rule. There was a large trail of people that would help this child, but they were only sworn in their hearts to do so. So far, no child had been lost that was in the care of the group at their church.

As she stepped into her car, Linda could hear sirens in the distance. They seemed to be coming nearer, but wanting to be early to work, she took no notice. She started the engine and backed out of her driveway. As she proceeded through her neighborhood, she began to put the sirens and the smoke in the sky together. She was only a few blocks away from her own home when she saw the fire. The Porter's house was ablaze. It was a horrifying sight; flames could be seen coming from the top of the house and through upstairs windows. Linda instinctively stopped. She knew the Porters. They had a teenage daughter named Emily. Linda had bought school fundraisers from Emily over the years, even talked to her about her plans to be a nurse someday, as well.

Suddenly, she saw Emily's dad run from the house carrying a small dog and supporting his wife who was screaming.

Linda left her car there in the driveway, thinking that it was far enough away to try to help. When she opened the car door, she realized that Mrs. Porter was screaming Emily's name. Emily was still in the house. Mr. Porter dropped their dog and ran back inside to find her. Mrs. Porter fell to the ground, overcome with smoke and panic. As she lay on the ground, Linda gave her CPR and stayed with her. Emergency services began to arrive. However, no Mr. Porter or Emily were in sight. Linda began to fear the very worst. The sight and smells of the home burning were overwhelming. The sight of seeing Mrs. Porter loaded into an ambulance, still unconscious, the helpless little dog being scooped up by a loving neighbor. The sobbing of friends who now were fearing that Mr. Porter and Emily were lost to the fire. Linda felt tears roll down her cheeks.

Suddenly, one of the firemen yelled and directed attention to the side of the house. Mr. Porter trudged out of the smoke with Emily, unconscious, slung across his shoulder. Firemen and EMT's swarmed the two. Just as suddenly, Linda remembered that she, too, had a mission. She had to get to the clinic immediately. She had not realized how much time had gone by and now she was not early. She would have to rush to make it on time, to be there for Victoria.

She had trouble leaving the scene of the fire, questions from police, backing her car carefully around emergency vehicles.

She looked up in the rear view to see her face, blackened with smoke. She did her best to restore her appearance. She did not have time to go home, to change clothes. She prayed to the Lord that Pat Carter would not be called in as back up for this morning's procedure. Pat was strictly business and would administer the overdose of anesthesia with the thought that she was saving the child from being raised in a home without love, or from a life of sickness, as was Victoria's case or with anything with which she could anesthetize her own conscience.

Five minutes earlier, Victoria's mother placed her daughter in the arms of nurse Pat Carter. Victoria's mother was accompanied by her boyfriend who kept telling her that she was doing the right thing for Victoria. It would be better for everyone. As Victoria was taken from her mother, she began to cry. Pat had been trained to keep this time as brief as possible. As she carried Victoria out of the room, the baby reached over her shoulder and Pat heard her cry "Mommie," but Pat just kept on walking. When she entered the procurement room, she held Victoria, who was screaming for her mother now. The doctor and another nurse strapped the baby to the table and inserted an IV, which only made the baby scream even more. She was now coughing and gasping between cries for her mother, who by now was driving out of the parking lot. The IV began and the baby quieted. Within a minute or two the death dose would begin.

Linda was driving into the parking lot when she saw the woman and man drive away. Another vehicle was parked next to the clinic. She noticed it because it looked like a medical transport van. There was a man at the driver's seat. She knew that this was probably her contact. The windows were darkened, and she could not see his face. She knew that she would not. She would simply open the unlocked door and place the sleeping Victoria on the bed in the van. The driver would confirm the child's name, letting her know that the next phase of the plan to save Victoria was beginning. Linda was to turn away immediately and close the door.

Linda was alarmed at seeing Pat's car in the lot but thought that she had made it to the clinic in enough time to get things done. She had the "fixed" syringe in her pocket. When it was checked by the doctor, it would read what he expected, but it would actually contain less medication. Victoria would only be very heavily sedated. Hopefully, there would be enough sedation to last two hours. By then, others would be with her to help her begin to make the adjustment to her new life.

As she opened the back door to the clinic, to her horror, Pat was wheeling out Victoria's lifeless body on a gurney under a plain white sheet. The body, along with a packet of papers containing Victoria's birth certificate and a copy of the procurement for the mortician were lying on top of the little body. It would be cremated. Her life would be erased.

"But not her soul, but not her soul," thought Linda. The outline of the little girl's body made it very hard to contain her tears.

The sound of Pat's voice snapped her mind back to consciousness.

"I know that this was supposed to be your case, this morning, but the parent arrived earlier than expected and Dr. Beckham made the decision....

Linda didn't hear the rest. She muttered okay and something about needing to go home because of the fire at neighbors and change her clothes...

She left out the same back door and walked to the back of the van. She opened the door and said only to the driver that there had been a horrible mistake. The child was already dead. When she said this, the driver turned, and she saw his face. She knew that face. It was Elizabeth Connally's chauffeur. He often helped Mrs. Connally into the church on Sunday. Their eyes met and she shut the door of the van, saying nothing.

There was nothing left to say. She sobbed all the way home.

When she got there, her Bible was still on the table. She read the words of the scripture again, but it would be later in the day before they comforted her heart.

Later that evening, as she lay in her bed, tears rolling down her cheeks, she told herself that it was God who spoke a word, engineered a circumstance... God and He only who had the power over life and death. It was His will that

weaved in and out of this day. Today... Emily lived
... Victoria died. She looked at Victoria's picture
on the file that lay beside her. She envisioned the
child in the arms of Jesus. She surrendered her
will to God. This was her new song to sing unto
the Lord. His will be done on earth as in heaven.

Finally, blessed sleep overtook her.

CHAPTER ELEVEN

CELENA AWOKE TO THE sound of her phone ringing early on Monday morning. She noticed as she reached for the phone on the bedside table, that the time said 5:00 a.m. She saw Merilee's face on the screen and knew what she probably wanted. She answered and Merilee with a strange calmness said that Dawson was very sick and needed to go to the clinic this morning to see the doctor. Celena knew that Dawson had been ill off and on with chronic ear infections, but she thought he was doing better. Merilee said that she would take Dawson to the clinic and then to her mother's house and come into work by noon. Celena told her that, of course, she would go to work today to help them. Merilee got off the phone quickly, for which Celena breathed a prayer of thanks. She called Mrs. Reiner and woke a disappointed Gracie who wanted to be with her Mommie all day on her day off. Celena thought it strange that Mrs. Reiner was already up and sounded very alert at such an early time of the morning but dismissed it and went on rushing around to get things ready for her day.

Celena could not have known that Mrs. Reiner had already received a phone call from Linda that woke her from a sound sleep. There was to be another procurement this morning, a four-year-old boy. There was some sort of rush to carry out the procedure because the boy would soon age out of the window of time allowed for procurement by his parents. Christmas holidays were approaching, and clinic hours would be adjusted. The mother wanted to go ahead with the release as soon as possible. There was no father listed on the birth certificate to object, so the procedure was pushed up to 10:00 a.m. this morning.

Mrs. Reiner spoke calmly assuring Linda that she would make the call to her contact as soon as they hung up the phone. Linda was still very shaken after the last procurement procedure. She was not sure her heart could stand another one with such an outcome. They prayed together and asked God to guide their footsteps this morning and help them preserve this child's life.

After they hung up, Mrs. Reiner called Rose Barton who was the group's coordinator and the only person who knew that William Hudson was the driver for all rescue transports. Hudson responded that it was his day off and he would pick up the van from the storage facility and be at the clinic by 10:00 a.m. that morning. Rose and William prayed together on the phone, asking God to make their way clear to the next church group who would allow time and help for Dawson to recover and then be transferred again to a third group many miles away for placement with a caring family. Some placements were even made outside the country. These required extra planning and incorporated greater risk. Everyone in the process played a vital role in the saving of a life. Each group of individuals took considerable risk by interfering with what was law in their country. It was an unabideable law, an effrontery to their faith. Only God held power over life and death. They worked to give those who had been murdered by their own parents a second chance at living. That was what was going to take place today. A chance to save a precious life.

Merilee was silent on the ride to the clinic. Dawson was playing a game on her phone and did not speak. She felt only coldness, numbness. Her mother's voice was ringing in her ears, telling her that she would stop the procurement. Merilee did not notice until she turned into the clinic parking lot that she was gripping the steering wheel until her knuckles had turned white.

When the door opened to receive them, Pat Carter asked her to come to a small inner office to sign the last set of final procurement papers and designate who would pick up the child's ashes from the crematorium. All procurements were cremated. This was the law.

The clinic used a private driver, Robert Calhoun, to transport bodies to funeral homes. Robert Calhoun and William Hudson were one and the same.

Robert would pick up the body by 11:00 a.m. He would transfer the child to a gurney in the back of his van. He began life-saving fluids provided by the church's pharmacy contact and administered with his expertise as an army medic in his early years. As the child began to revive to a sleeping state rather than unconscious, he quickly drove to the church where at least two group members would be waiting to fill the "PROCUREMENT" box which Dawson was put into after his "death" with the exact weight of his body. They used scraps of Percy's food hidden in the freezer by Hudson to provide weight for the transfer box. These scraps had been prepared so that there would be ashes in the box but not human ones. The box would be sealed with heavy-duty tape and taken to the facility for cremation. Body Boxes could be opened by facilities, but Hudson had never seen that happen, perhaps because of the contents of the box. No one wanted to view a child killed by procurement, at least not so far. Hudson had no contingency plan for this, should it happen. He relied on prayer that God would intervene.

Pat summoned Linda who was to take over when the young procurement arrived. Linda was prepared. She took Dawon by the hand and walked him into the procedure room. She helped him crawl up the steps on the examination table. He asked where his mother was, and Linda said truthfully that she was still in the small office with the other nurse. She gave Dawson a lollypop laced with anesthetic. Standard procedure for children four years of age and older. It worked amazingly quick. Dawson was sleeping within about five minutes. No crying, no screaming when the IV was placed in his arm. The presiding doctor came in and noted Dawson's heart-rate and pulse, signed the procurement release as attending physician. He examined the IV and saw the syringe filled with the final dose that would kill Dawson painlessly, quickly. He lingered for a moment longer than usual which alarmed Linda, but he did not like this part of his job and soon left the room to let Linda administer the life-taking dose and bear the direct responsibility.

I guess he sleeps better that way, she thought.

Linda administered the syringe. She waited five minutes and then took the death certificate to the doctor to sign. Indeed, Dawson appeared lifeless and almost was. Linda needed to move quickly now, so that the driver could administer fluids containing medicine that would alter Dawson's state of unconsciousness and let him sleep off the ordeal, peacefully in the back of the transport van.

The doctor signed the death certificate. Linda loaded Dawson's unconscious body into the box labeled "PROCUREMENT" and rolled the box on its gurney to the back door. The driver was waiting. She knew to turn around after leaving the body on the back porch entrance. The driver would do the rest.

Hudson rolled the gurney to the back of the van and loaded Dawson into the back. He shut the door and went back to the driver's side. No one could see that the process was beginning inside the van. The process that would continue to save Dawson's life.

CHAPTER 12

MERILEE SWERVED HER CAR into the parking lot of the small store where she and Celena worked. She had been drinking from a flask in her purse since early this morning, right after she left Dawson at the clinic.

She came in the door like thunder to find Celena checking out cigarettes for a customer. She tripped over a display of magazines and fell to the floor. Celena and the customer helped Merilee up and her drunkenness was obvious to them both. Celena helped Merilee sit down behind the counter as the customer left.

"You're drunk, Merilee," said Celena.

"No, just drinking," slurred Merilee and continued to babble something about Dawson, but Celena could not understand her.

"You have got to get out of here before Rose finds you like this," she warned, "you could lose your job."

Celena hated to leave the store to take Merilee back to her car, but there did not seem another option. There was no time to find someone to drive her home. Celena knew how badly she needed to keep her job. She thought that Merilee was the same. Merilee made it to her car and Celena felt a little better when she saw her drive out of the parking lot without hitting a curb and stopping at the street corner. Celena did not know that when she stopped, she took out her flask and finished it off. Anything to deaden the pain, the guilt that she was beginning to feel. She had begun to remember times spent with Dawson. Days at the park. She remembered how he laughed at everything. All of a sudden, and maybe for the first time, she felt that she was a part of him and now his death was a part of her. She never saw the red light. She heard the brakes screech and then the crash, and then nothing.

From within the store, Celena could hear sirens and surmised that something had happened at the nearby intersection. Rose had heard the commotion too and motioned for Celena to take a look outside.

Celena donned her coat and went out the door to discover to her horror that it was Merilee's car that had been virtually run over by a large truck. Celena screamed and ran toward the accident. Rose closed the shop and followed. As she walked toward the intersection, she wondered how anyone in the car beneath the truck could have survived. She whispered a prayer for Merilee.

Both women stood as paramedics pulled the truck driver from his vehicle. They could see Merilee slumped inside the car. When they were finally able to remove her from her car, she appeared lifeless. One paramedic began to try to resuscitate her. He was still working on her as she was loaded into the ambulance.

Rose and Celena walked back to Rose's car and drove to the hospital in silence.

When they got there, the emergency room doctor motioned them around to the small room where Merilee was. He had thought that perhaps they were family. He shook his head and the grim look on his face prepared them for the bad news. Merilee would probably not survive long enough to get to surgery. Rose told him that they were Merilee's friends and could summon her parents. Celena knew Merilee's mother's name and still had the number in her phone from an earlier visit with Mrs. Cooper. She stepped out of Merilee's room and made the call. Rose took a small silver cross from her purse and bent low over Merilee. Celena could see Rose's lips moving and assumed that she was praying. After Celena made the tragic call to the Coopers, she returned to Merilee's bedside and was surprised to find that she had regained consciousness. She was looking straight at Rose who was talking to Merilee about Jesus. Merilee told Rose the terrible thing that she did that morning and that it was unforgiveable. Her breaths were very short and ragged. Celena could hear the gurgling in her chest. Merilee did not have long. Rose unshakingly testified that if Merilee asked Jesus into her heart right now, that all sins not just this morning, but for her whole life had been paid for on the cross. Merilee nodded, no longer able to speak. Her blue eyes became clear and wide, as though she was seeing something no one else in the room could see. The nurse rushed in as the monitor alarm sounded.

"Keep talking to her, she can still hear you," said the kindhearted nurse.

Rose bent near to Merilee's ear and whispered, "Dawson is alive!"

Merilee smiled, eyes wide open and died.

Dawson, Dawson, she had not thought of Dawson until now and was frightened for him. Merilee's mom and dad arrived and the doctor began speaking in a soft voice to try to help them understand what had happened to their daughter. Mrs. Cooper broke down into Mr. Cooper's arms and thanked God that Dawson had not been in the car.

Confusion ensued about where Dawson could be. The only person in the room that knew could say nothing. The next few days would be extremely hard for the Cooper's. They would find procurement papers in Merilee's effects and would be devastated by her loss and his. Celena would learn what happened to Dawson, and it would break her heart, at least initially. There were a lot of changes coming in her life, too.

Celena snapped back to the present and remembered that it was time to pick up Gracie. She called Jack. She wasn't sure if it was because he worked close by in the neighborhood and knew Mrs. Reiner or because she just needed to hear his voice. He answered his phone and said that he would pick up Gracie and wait for Celena at their apartment. She thanked him and she and Rose left Merilee for the last time.

When they reached the store, Rose took Celena by the shoulders turning her where they were face to face. She knew for sure about Celena, now. She knew where she stood in her belief in God. Celena lived her faith. She was always loyal, always compassionate, caring so much for Merilee who was hardened by her life until the moment before death. Celena was genuinely happy that Merilee accepted Jesus Christ into her heart repenting of her sins. Merilee was in Heaven now.

Celena was ready and Rose was ready to tell her about the Church group that was saving lives at great risk. She began slowly by asking Celena about her faith in God.

Celena told Rose that she had been saved at the age of seven.

She grew up in a Christian home with loving parents.

"With all these blessings, I managed to make a mess of my life in high school. I was wild, drinking and running with a crowd that was mostly godless. I met Jack when I was nineteen and we married against my parents' wishes. I thought we would straighten each other out, that Gracie would help us to grow up and make a family. Gracie saved me but she couldn't bring Jack around," explained Celena.

"Gracie didn't save you, honey. Only Jesus saves. God gave you Gracie as the natural blessing of your marriage to Jack," replied Rose.

As Celena began to cry, it was like walking home from a long day's journey. She told Rose how her heart was broken, not just from her separation from Jack, but the distance she had put between herself and her parents, herself and Jesus. She wanted to come full circle, back to her faith, back to her parents, back to God.

The two women knelt and prayed in the store asking Jesus to rule in Celena's heart again bringing her hope and sweet peace. They prayed that God would somehow let Merilee know in Heaven that her acceptance of salvation had meant so much to Celena, too.

Rose told Celena that Dawson was not dead, but indeed alive and beginning a new life with a family far from here. Celena's heart was over-come with this joyful knowledge. She threw her arms around Rose's neck and thanked her.

"Don't thank me. Praise God... and join us," said Rose.

Celena nodded because her joyful sobs would not let her speak.

When she got home later that night, she turned her key in the door and opened it to find Jack and Gracie asleep on the sofa with the television still on. She sat down beside Jack, waking him. Neither of them moved off the sofa or apart from one another for about an hour. They talked softly so as not to wake their daughter.

They talked about the past and Karen and how it changed their lives. Celena and Jack both realized that they were at a crossroads in their lives and in their marriage. Jack asked for Celena's foregiveness and now she was able to give it. They made a pact to stay together and raise their child. Jack made promises to Celena that he would not have been able to make before. Celena forgave him and accepted the promises that she would never have been able to accept without the lifechanging love of Jesus in her heart.

Jack carried Gracie to her bed. He kissed Celena and left to return tomorrow to the home he was now a part of again.

Celena lay next to Gracie in her little bed. She listened to Gracie's slow, even breaths. She prayed asking God to always stay with her, just as He had been all the time these past months. Celena had never been alone. God was always watching and protecting her. She prayed God's protection over Gracie, too.

CHAPTER 13

BETH LOWERY WAS GLAD to be home with her parents and new little brother for the holidays. She was completing her second year in training to be a nurse at both the hospital and the local nursing school, which was about an hour's drive from her parents' home. Beth had taken a week's vacation at her mom's request to come back home for a few days after Christmas. June and Brian Lowery wanted Beth to meet her new brother, but they had other reasons to see their daughter, as well. Very important things had to be discussed with Beth, now.

June Lowery would be telling Beth about her procurement.

"Good morning," said her mother as Beth sat down at the breakfast table.

Dawson, her newly adopted brother, was also sitting at the table. He had been quiet since his parents picked him up last week. Beth could see that he did not sleep well the night before. She reached across the table and ruffled his hair. When he did not respond, she got up, bent over him and kissed him on top of the head.

"It's gonna be okay, buddy" she said, trying to comfort him.

Beth remembered that she was about the same age when she was adopted by the Lowerys. It was a while before the world turned right side up for her too, but eventually, it did.

The Lowerys were so loving and patient with her. Her mom and dad waited for love to grow in her heart for them, and it certainly did.

Beth got up and helped her mother finish the eggs and bacon. She took the biscuits out of the oven and helped Dawson put some butter on a biscuit for himself. She asked him if he liked grape jelly. To this sweet question, Dawson gave his first smile and said "Yes ma,am."

Beth smiled at him and told him that she was his sister and just an "okay" was good enough.

Dawson ate his breakfast today and this made Mr. and Mrs. Lowery smile, too. He had spoken little, was still very sad and not open to any interaction with them. He still cried for his mother at night. It was heartbreaking for the Lowerys, but this was not their first procurement child. With time and lots of love and patience, Dawson would come around.

It would be a good year ahead for Dawson.

It would be a challenging year for Beth.

Brian Lowery took Dawson outside to look at the snow that had begun gently falling. June Lowery took Beth by the arm and led her to the living room where the sound of the crackling fireplace seemed so warm and welcoming.

"Honey, your father and I have something to tell you about yourself that we have waited to share with you until this time."

June began Beth's story as she quietly listened. June told Beth about her arriving at their home in the middle of the night about twenty years ago. She went on to tell her that her adoption was a bit unusual. A year after Beth's arrival, the family moved to another part of the country, a brand new home in a brand new place. The home that they live in now.

Beth was sensitive enough to realize that her mother was going somewhere with all of this, so she continued to quietly listen.

June told her that she was a child of "procurement" and that through the love of Christians who did not know her, her life was saved, and she was moved away to another life where she would survive and thrive.

"That's where we came into your life, Beth."

As a nurse, Beth knew what "procurement" meant. The Lowerys never said anything about her birth parents and Beth had never asked. She had wondered as a teen about who they might be, but her life was happy. She was always busy with school, sports, church and family. Her parents were the Lowerys. It was enough for her.

Beth was a grown woman now, but news that her biological mother had, in a sense, killed her was overwhelming. She sat in silence. June continued, "there's more, if you can hear it, honey."

Beth only nodded.

June went on to tell her that as they agreed twenty years before when they welcomed Beth into their family, she would be told about her history and given the choice to seek out any biological relatives from her past.

That was enough. Beth needed a few minutes to take it all in.

"I'm going to go get you another cup of coffee and give you some time to think about all this," said June.

While in the kitchen, June washed the dishes and made a fresh pot of coffee before going back to her daughter.

She came back to Beth with two cups of coffee for the two of them. She sat down across from Beth. She expected tears or anger. Instead, Beth spoke calmly, evenly, smiling at her mother. "Mom, you and Dad are my parents, and Dawson is my new brother. This is my family. This is my life. I don't want to go back." Mother and daughter embraced. The tears flowed now, but they were tears of pure joy.

I just have one question. "Is Dawson the result of procurement, too?" Beth asked.

"Yes," replied June.

"Let's go out and look at the snow with Dawson and Dad," Beth said.

CHAPTER 14

THE CHURCH SOCIAL PLANNING Committee commenced its monthly meeting on a bright spring day in April. Rose called the meeting to order, and they began to discuss new business which included a bake sale and a gathering for a potluck meal in May for all members of the church. These matters were dispatched quickly, and Rose called on Linda Norris for a report about the more challenging business at hand.

Linda reported that there had been four requests for procurements since January. Two had been rescinded and two had proceeded. One child had been rescued. One child had not, to her great sadness.

The group paused and Linda led a prayer for this child that they were unable to rescue. She asked for God's mercy and guidance for the group. She also sought God's protection for them as they tried to save as many as they could.

When the meeting resumed. The group discussed letting Elizabeth Connally know that her granddaughter had been rescued many years ago. Several months had gone by since Beth had been been told by her family that she had been rescued, and indeed, had living family members with whom she could connect if she wished. As Nola Reiner pointed out, she would probably have already contacted Lizzie by now. She added that it would also relieve Lizzie's long suffering just to know that Beth was alive.

"At least, she could stop agonizing over an empty grave," she concluded.

The group decided unanimously that Nola Reiner would give Lizzie the news.

New members to the group, Jack and Celena Garrett, were welcomed and allowed to vote in today's proceedings. Celena, who was now expecting their second child spoke for both of them by saying that she and Jack were happy to be accepted into the group and were praying that God would use them to help save the lives of procured children in the future.

Just as they were about to adjourn, the door opened slowly. Elizabeth Connally walked down the steps and took her seat at the table. She was escorted by her granddaughter, Beth Lowery. She introduced Beth to the group. There were tears and hugs and much joy.

Beth asked to join the group. She explained that she would be on the nursing staff at a local clinic. She was looking for a home in the area and would be staying with her grandmother until then. Beth said that she wanted to give others the chance that she was given. Her membership was granted.

Full circle had finally come through Beth Lowery. Hopefully, others would follow.

Until then, God's grace and mercy would be sufficient for them all.

The End

www.ingramcontent.com/pod-product-compliance
Lightning Source LLC
Chambersburg PA
CBHW070828250626
47170CB00006B/2254